What Angels Fear?

Play to Screen
by
Alex P. Michaels

What Angels Fear?

Play to Screen
by
Alex P. Michaels

3

About the Author

Emmy winning writer and award winning director, Alex has produced a number of ind
movies and a TV series in his hometown of Cleveland, Ohio. He founded the Movie ar
Marketing Company Prelude2Cinema. Although Prelude2Cinema shoots in Northeast, Ohi
its movies have played all over the world. Alex also acts in other movies from othe
directors. Alex is the Cinema Czar and dedicated to creating a Cinema Industry
Northeast Ohio that is based on the old Hollywood Studio System and promotes movie
and includes Hollywood and Indie filmmakers.

"For Bobby Dunlap"

Table of Contents

ear Friend,

about 4am as I write this. I am always still staying up late at night. I want to thank you for ying this book and I want to be open with you about how it all begun. Since we are friends, I n share things with you.

the time I wrote this, I was still working at the hospital with the dreams of being a doctor d writing books that would become so successful that a Hollywood director would want to e it over. I wasn't planning to direct but I had dabbled with it after "The Hot Rain." Yet, that's other story for another time.

ot burned out. This was right after the little crazy Polish girl Yvette. She had been sick and so pent a lot time in the hospital seeing her before and after my shift. I remember going in at m to see her, working at 7am, seeing her at lunch and in between the day, then if I didn't work double, I'd stay with her till she fell asleep. I repeated that for the weeks she was in the spital.

always loved film noir and growing up with it, most of my stories were like that. I had eated a cop named Lt. Foster who turns up in a number of different stories.

rying to keep focused here. Ahh, that is the problem. Never could focus on more than one ing at a time. After Yvette and I imploded and the hospital got too much to bear, I had moved om patient transport to patient assistance and studying medicine, one day I just left work and t on a plane and went to live with my brother in California.

hose days were kind of like an old movie, where a writer from the midwest packs it up and aves to Hollywood to make his fortune. Well, it wasn't exactly Hollywood, but up north in alifornia and with no contacts in the business, I just wrote all day or took long walks and had ushi or hung out in a book store.

ly brother lived in a place called Redwood City and behind his apartment was a ditch and then her apartments across the way. One day, walking out, I got a "vision." That is the way I write ometimes. I believe the stories I write are "out there in some other reality, and I just am able to ee them." Well, at least at that time I did believe that and maybe I still do to a sense. So, I get is "vision" of these two cops getting caught in a crossfire between cops and drug dealers. I adn't planned to write a cop story then and I was working on "The Hot Rain." A love story. ome true. Some not but the cop story was just that one vision.

shrugged it off and when I got back home, there was this contest "The Dreambuilder's elebration." A talented white director named Jim Friedman formed a contest to help black vriters. I submitted "The Hot Rain," an interracial love story that I loved and wanted to come ee to the screen.

It was rejected.

So, I decided to make the movie myself. It was a play that I first staged at the Karamu House, historic black theater.

Still, the cop story stuck with me. There was also a news article about some Cleveland Cops who were less than honest. That became part of the story. Yet in my story, the cops weren't just doing it for greed, like in real life. They were doing it because they wanted a better life for the family and was tired of risking their life for little money while the drug dealers made fortunes.

I wish I could remember all the details of how I wrote this story and when I decided to put Lt. Foster in it. He shows up in other stories of mine. Which I hope to share with you soon. His being in the story, which I titled "What Angels Fear?" became the anchor for it.

I staged a reading at Karamu House by entering it into a festival of new plays.

Later when "The Dreambuilder's Celebration" was looking for scripts for its second year, I entered "What Angels Fear?"

This time, I won.

So friends, here is the story that started it all. In a sense. I hope we get to "talk more." You can find me online if you want to talk about this story or anything in this letter.

Thanks for buying my story. Thanks for reading this letter and reading my story. Thanks for being a friend.

Sincerely,
Alex P. Michaels
https://www.facebook.com/alex.p.michaels

http://prelude2cinema.com/alex-p-michaels/

What Angels Fear? The Play

by
Alex P. Michaels

A ROOM OF AN ABANDONED HOUSE AND KEVIN

BOCHELLI'S HOUSE

The set is divided. Near the back of upstage left
is a couch that is in the living room of KEVIN'S
house. Behind this is the exit which leads to the
kitchen and to the upstairs bedroom. The dining
table near downstage right is in an abandoned
house, but will later be used as the dining room
of KEVIN's house. At the back wall of upstage
right is the door to the abandoned house and a
few boxes are sitting there. A light is on the
table and a separate light is on KEVIN's living
room. The action in the first scene goes on at
the same time, but in different places across
town.

SCENE ONE: ABANDONED HOUSE

TWO BLACK MEN enter the abandoned house. One is
SLY. He is wearing a dark suit and moves with an
arrogant but friendly air. The other is a huge
man named J. He looks nervous, but in control. He
is carrying a suitcase and puts it on the table.
The two are carrying on a conversation that begin
outside.

At the same time, KEVIN comes from upstage left.
He is a thirtysomething White Man who is not ugly
or handsome, just average. He is carrying a
similar suitcase and a children's book. His
twelve year old daughter JESSICA (JIMMIE) is
riding piggyback. Her smile makes her prettier
than she really is. He carefully sits her down on
the couch, then he sits down himself. She crawls
into his arms and he begins to read from the book
to her. She is wearing blue pajamas and he is
wearing a dark suit.

SLY sits at the table. J comes to the center of
the stage and looks out at the audience.

J

As a black man, I have been
lied to about the importance
of education. Fredrick
Douglas believed that
education was the key to
freedom. At the time, it was,
and for a lot of us it still
remains that way. Money and
power eludes me. It is money
and power which dictates what
kind of home we can live in.
It allows us a neighborhood
where our children can play
outside without fear of being
accosted by drug dealers. I
believe that the right to
consume drugs is a choice
made by adults. I do not prey
on children.

Some of my other colleagues
do.
The question put to every
black man is "What are you
doing to further the race?"
You never hear a White guy
say, "Hey, Charlie, your new
yacht really moves the white
race ahead in a positive
way." I am doing like the
White Man. I am furthering
myself. I am gaining power. I
am acquiring money and a
status of fear. I believe
with that I can reach the
American dream. A few weeks
ago, a boat load of Haitians
and Cubans died just trying
to get to America. You can
bet your ass they wanted the
American dream.

Power and money is the American dream. I told this young recruit that legality is made by the politicians. Look at nicotine and caffeine; two of the most addictive drugs, but acceptable in this society, therefore, legal. I've seen people almost knock me down trying to get into a coffee house. Their eyes are wired, their hand is shaking and they will tell you, "They can't get through the day without that first cup." If caffeine was outlawed, you'd see business men on the street. "You got some espresso beans. Just a taste, man, just a taste." People would go to the same desperate measures that they did when alcohol was illegal. How many people lost their lives with that experiment? Selling drugs is the only thing left for the Black Man. It's the only thing left for me. The White Man has forced us to kill ourselves in order to attain power. To attain money, I have to sell drugs that I know will kill people. I can't curb their desires and I would be a humanitarian fool to not take advantage of it. I could work in a job for twenty years and hope that the White Man over looks his own natural desire and favoritism and gives me the much deserved promotion over his nephew, but let's be honest with ourselves. Drugs

are the key to power. To the
American dream that has
eluded us. If I don't take
advantage of the desire by
others to kill themselves,
then someone else will.
Besides a lot of my clients
are rich white kids who are
rebelling because their Daddy
bought them a BMW instead of
a Mercedes.

(J goes over to the case. He opens the case and
places one of the bags of white powder against
his cheek.)

                    J
          I think it's ironic about the
          color. That the color of our
          salvation is white.

(Lights fade on J as he sits at the table and
begins to talk to SLY. KEVIN is reading to
JIMMIE. He stops reading. She looks at him.
JIMMIE goes before the couch and moves into the
classic position to pray.)

SCENE TWO: THE BOCHELLI'S LIVING ROOM

Lights come up on KEVIN and JIMMIE.

(KEVIN sits the suitcase on the couch and watches
JIMMIE.)

                  JIMMIE
          Now, I lay me down to sleep.
          I pray the Lord my soul to
          keep. If I should die before
          I wake, I pray the Lord my
          soul to take. Uhhmm God, this
          is Jessica Bochelli... You
          know, Jimmie. Please watch
          out for Daddy tonight when he
          goes to work and watch out
          for Uncle Sly... and Foster.
          And I promise to eat anything

nasty that Mommy finds in
that cookbook. Amen.

(KEVIN opens the case. It is full of stacks of
twenties. He pulls one out of the case and flicks
through it. He does this with the others and
takes a moment with one to let it rub against his
cheek.)
                    (

                    JIMMIE
          God, it must be a billion
          dollars in there.

                    KEVIN
          Not by a long shot. It's
          enough to keep us comfortable
          for a long time. You have to
          remember, money can't buy
          everything, but who wants
          everything. It sure can buy a
          lot. We could use a lot.

(Behind them near the "door" leading to the
kitchen and upstairs, MIKI BOCHELLI enters. She
is wearing a simple house dress and may have been
pretty once, but now she just looks tired. She
stays in the background watching her husband and
daughter.)JIMMIE stands and turns to KEVIN. She
walks over to the case and looks down in it.)

                    KEVIN
          What do you want me to buy
          you when I go out?

                    JIMMIE
          A Ferrari.

                    KEVIN
          You can't drive.

                    JIMMIE
          So buy me a driver too. He's
          got to be good looking and
          speak Spanish.

                    KEVIN
          Ohh, I got to keep my eyes on
          you, Young Lady.

                    JIMMIE
          Can I touch it?

(She puts her hand out to the money. Kevin takes
a stack out of the pile and puts it in her hand.
He pulls her to him. He puts his arms around her
from behind so that he is holding onto her and
the money in her hand.)

                    KEVIN
          That is something that will
          get us places. It's
          opportunity. I mean, I use to
          think it was just money. It
          was just something to use to
          pay the mortgage and the
          bills, but it's a lot more
          than that. It's-

                    JIMMIE
          What's a mortgage?

                    KEVIN
          It's a bill. It means someone
          else owns this house and we
          have to pay them money or
          they'll kick us out on the
          street.

                    JIMMIE
          When are they going to kick
          us out?

                    KEVIN
          Don't worry baby, soon, we'll
          have a lot of this stuff and
          we can buy this place. Hey,
          we might even get a bigger
          house. One day soon.

                    MIKI
          Jessica.

(JIMMIE stops and looks at her Mother. MIKI walks
over and stands behind the couch. She reaches
over and closes the case. She looks JIMMIE in the
eye.)

                    MIKI
          Go to your room.

                    JIMMIE
          Now?

                    MIKI
          No, two seconds ago.

(She hugs KEVIN.)

                    JIMMIE
          Night Daddy.

(She moves behind the couch and hugs MIKI.)

                    JIMMIE
          Night Mommy.

(JIMMIE looks over her shoulder at the case.)

                    KEVIN
          Jimmie.

(She walks around the couch. He points at the
stack of twenties she is holding in her hand. He
takes it from her.)

                    JIMMIE
          Goodnight billion dollars.

(JIMMIE runs off.)

                    JIMMIE
          Don't forget my Ferrari,
          Daddy.

(JIMMIE disappears behind the curtain at upstage
left. MIKI comes to the other side of the couch
and looks down at KEVIN. He stands and takes the
case with him.)

                    KEVIN
I got to go meet Sly.

                    MIKI
You Son of a bitch.

                    KEVIN
What?

                    MIKI
Why did you let her see that?

                    KEVIN
It popped open. She knows
what I do, Miki. She always
has. Okay. Now, I got to go
to work.

                    MIKI
Yeah. She knows what you are,
but do you have to let her
touch it? You would have
never did that before, Kevin.
What was all that about,
money is opportunity. It's
going to take us places. What
was that-

                    KEVIN
What? Are you spying on me? I
can't spend time alone with
Jimmie lately without you
watching over my damn
shoulder every five minutes!

                    MIKI
Why are you yelling?

                    KEVIN
I wasn't yelling.

                    MIKI
Kevin, I'm not stupid. I know
when I'm being yelled at like
a little kid.

                    KEVIN
          It's not that. I wasn't doing
          that. Okay, okay, I'm sorry.
          I don't have time for this.
          We'll talk when I get back. I
          promise I won't let Jimmie
          see the money anymore.

                    MIKI
          You have a few minutes. You
          drive fast anyway.

                    KEVIN
          I can't drive but so fast.
               (smiling at her)
          If the cops catch me with
          this...

                    MIKI
          Don't worry about the cops.
          I'm worried about you. I'm
          worried about us. That's more
          important than the money or
          the cops. That's more ...
          That's the most important
          thing in my life.

                    KEVIN
          This is not the time.

(She takes the case and puts it behind her.)

                    MIKI
          What is this worth to you?

(He puts out his hand to the case and she moves
back.)

                    MIKI
          Can I have five minutes of
          your time?

(He sits on the couch. She opens the case and
takes out five stacks. She hands him the case.)

                    MIKI
          A stack per minute.

                    KEVIN
          Miki?

(She holds up one of the stacks.)

                    MIKI
          Kevin, I've never been scared
          to talk to you. I'm scared
          now. I see you with Jimmie
          and you're talking to her
          like you love this stuff.

(She tosses him one of the stacks. He catches it
and puts it in the case.)

                    KEVIN
          I was joking with her?

                    MIKI
          I know when you're joking.
          She's in there sleeping right
          now. She's going to be
          dreaming of a Ferrari. She
          can't even spell Ferrari.
          It's too easy to get seduced
          by this stuff. That's what I
          loved about you. You never
          cared about this stuff.

(She tosses him another stack.)

                    KEVIN
          Loved?

                    MIKI
          I still love you.

(He puts the case on the couch and stands up.)

                    KEVIN
          You said loved?

                    MIKI
          You know what I meant.

KEVIN

My mind is not on this
conversation. I know that
sounds mean, but I have to go
to work. I don't want to slip
up tonight. I can not think
about this now. I can not
have this discussion now.

(He grabs the rest of the money out of her hand.
He puts it in the case. He closes the case.)

MIKI

When can I talk to you?
You're never home.

KEVIN

I was here all day yesterday.
I didn't hear you say any of
this. I didn't hear you say a
damn thing.

MIKI

I wanted to Kevin. I wanted
to.

KEVIN

Look, can't this wait? Now
kiss me, please. I have to go
and I want to know we're okay
before I go.

(She lowers her head and he walks over to her.
Just as he is about to put his arms around her,
she smacks him.)

MIKI

If you ever show her a case
full of money and talk about
buying a Ferrari when we
can't even afford to pay the
mortgage, I will kick your
ass. As much as I love you, I
will hurt you Kevin. Is that
clear?

(He nods, then grabs her wrists and the case
drops to the floor.)

                        KEVIN
            You want me to bring you back
            anything while I'm out?

(She stands up and puts her hand on his
heart.)KEVIN sighs and gently pushes MIKI aside.
He stands up as she sits on the couch. He picks
up the case. He looks down at her.)He pulls her
to him and kisses her. He steps back from her.
She smiles at him. He smiles back.)

                        MIKI
            Just come home.

(He takes her hand and kisses it, then leaves.
KEVIN goes far downstage center then turns right
and walks behind the curtain at upstage right.
MIKI sits on the couch for a moment. She picks up
the children's book and looks at it. As the
lights fade on her, she goes back "upstairs".)

                        SLY
            He'll be here. He doesn't
            exactly live in this
            neighborhood.

                        J
            Oh, I'm certain of that. It's
            just, I like these things to
            be over with quickly. The
            quicker they move along, the
            less chance of something
            going wrong.

(There is a knock at the door.)Lights rises on
SLY and J. J is pacing back and forth. J walks
over to the table and picks up the case.)

                        SLY
            I knew Kevin wouldn't let me
            down.

                    J
          Well Kevin better not let me
          down.

(SLY goes to the door and returns with KEVIN. He
enters with the case at his side. J smiles as he
goes over and shakes his hand.)

                    J
          My friend, you are slightly
          over dressed. I trust the
          inhabitants of this
          neighborhood didn't see you
          as prey.

                 KEVIN
          I can be quite resourceful
          when I have to be.

                    J
          So, I've heard. Okay, let's
          commence.

(J leads SLY and KEVIN to the table. KEVIN places
his briefcase on the table. J places the other
briefcase on the table next to KEVIN's. They open
the cases at the same time. J's case is filled
with seven packets filled with coke. KEVIN's case
is filled with cash. J looks at KEVIN's case and
closes it. J nods and picks up the case. He
begins to walk toward the door.)
                    (

                 KEVIN
          J, don't you want to count
          it?

(J stops and turns to KEVIN. He sits the case on
the floor and walks up to KEVIN.)KEVIN closes J's
case and looks at J.)

                    J
          Why should I? I trust you.
          Besides, if it isn't all
          there, I'll hunt you down
          like a dog and kill you.

                    KEVIN
          Ah?

(He pats Kevin on his cheek. J walks to SLY. He
puts his hand on SLY'S shoulder.)

                     J
          Sly, call me. We'll do lunch
          at my little diner on the
          west side.

                    SLY
          I'd like that.

                     J
          Kevin, it's been a pleasure.
          Ask Sly to bring you to the
          diner. I can spend more time
          being friendly. I don't like
          to spend a lot of time doing
          business though. Good night.

(He opens the door.)

                  BLACK OUT
          SOUND of Cops bursting into
          the room.

                   VOICES
          Freeze. Get on the floor. Get
          on the damn floor. Don't move
          or I'll blow your damn head
          off...

(Sirens are heard screaming as the voices
continue. J, SLY and KEVIN move off stage. The
voices start to die down as the lights come back
up.)

FOSTER

Prayers are important. I
prayed before we came in. My
Mother told me that God would
always be with me, but it was
important that he know I
wanted him to be with me. My
Mother believes police are
Angels.My Mother was walking
home from the diner where she
worked. My Mother couldn't
afford to take the bus home
so she had to walk down
Prospect. A Man stepped out
of the night. They always
come out of the night. He saw
her short skirt. Her boss
insisted she wear short
skirts. It would make the
people buy more. Well, a
woman alone at night on the
street in a short dress. It
brings images to a Man's
mind. This Man told her what
he wanted. What he would pay.
She tried to walk away from
him and he kept following her
waving the money. "Come on,
Honey," he said, "I know you
need it. It'll be fun." There
was a guy coming out of a
drug store walking toward my
Mother and the Man. My Mother
tells the Man bothering her
that all she wants to do is
get home to her kids. The Man
says, "Bitch, I offered to
pay for it, now I'm just
going to take it for free."
The Man grabs her. My Mother
looks at the guy who came out
of the drug store. She says,
"God, please help me." The

Man who is holding her laughs. He says, "Honey, this guy ain't gonna help you. Nobody helps anybody. Nobody cares about anybody." He turns to the guy and says, "Ain't that right, buddy?" The guy shakes his head and pulls out a gun and puts it to the Man's head. The Man lets go of my Mother. My Mother looks at the guy holding the gun on the Man. She says, "Who are you?" He says his name is Angel. Officer Angel.

I was only five years old when Angel brought my Mother home. I was up playing, but I was suppose to be asleep. All I heard was voices in the living room. My Mother sounded like a little girl talking, trying not to cry. Angel's voice sounded as if it was from heaven. He told her to calm down. "There was no need to be afraid. There was nothing to fear."

She asked him was he on duty that evening. He said, No. He had a bad cold and he stopped to get some cough drops. He was praying that he would get over the cold. God puts you where you need to be. I remember his voice. It was so gentle.

I had to see him before he left. I ran out of my room to see him. He was ugly. He was overweight, balding. His nose looked like it had been broken more than once. He looked down at me. I was a

little kid. You know the
type, says the first thing on
my mind. I said, you're funny
looking. My Mother was about
to die.

(Foster smiles to himself.)

                FOSTER
My Mother couldn't believe
it. The Man had just saved
her life. Angel, he... Angel
just laughed. He put his hand
on my shoulder. He said, in
that voice, in that angelic
voice, "You're right. I am
funny looking. Everyone knows
that. My Mom even says I'm
funny looking.
He puts his hand on my heart
and smiled at me and left. He
was ugly, but his voice was
beautiful.
1st Samuel chapter 16 verse 7
says "For the LORD seeth not
as man, for man looketh on
the outward appearance, but
the LORD looketh on the
heart." I have a beautiful
heart. God gave me that.
That's why I'm a cop. It's
better to be ugly and have a
beautiful heart, than to be
beautiful and have an ugly
heart. My Mother told me
Angel... police had no fears.
For a long while I believed
her. Till I became a cop, I
believed her. They had no
fears. I wonder if she could
see me now, what would she
think. I was shaking when we
came in. Whenever we pull out
our guns, I have my fears
something will go wrong. It

                     only takes one pound of
                     pressure to pull a trigger.
                     One finger and all hell could
                     break lose.

(pause)
                     Okay, I need a drink.

(FOSTER walks to the door and leaves.

SCENE: A DINER ACROSS FROM THE POLICE STATION

SLY comes back in and sits at the table. He has
one of the suitcases with him. KEVIN comes in and
sits with him. KEVIN is carrying a plate of
donuts. KEVIN leaves for a moment and returns
with two cups of coffee. He hands one to SLY.)

                     SLY
              Damn, I am glad that's over.

                     KEVIN
              Unn huh?

                     SLY
              So what did Miki make for
              dinner? We can do the reports
              at your house.

(KEVIN slides the case over to him and opens it.
he looks inside, counts, and closes the case.
KEVIN sits back.)A SINGLE COP walks in and stands
in the center of the room. This is FOSTER. He is
a tall Black man wearing a suit under his trench
coat. His face is serene.)

                     SLY
              You know it's funny, J seems
              like a real intelligent guy.
              We had lunch and he was
              talking to me about when he
              was a college student. He did
              this paper on drug dealers
              and he got enthralled in the `
              life style. I hated being
              with the guy. I just kept

                    thinking what you told me,
                    when we joined the force.

(KEVIN is still looking at the case. He opens it
and counts it again and closes the case.)

                         SLY
                    "Just because someone is evil
                    doesn't mean they aren't
                    intelligent. That's what
                    makes them truly evil. How
                    smart they are. Hitler was
                    intelligent. He was also
                    evil." I think Jay is...
                    Kevin?

(KEVIN is still looking at the case. He opens it
and is starting to count.)

                         SLY
                    Kevin!

(KEVIN stops, closes the case and looks at SLY.)

                         SLY
                    What is it? Did you hear
                    anything I was saying?

                         KEVIN
                    Yeah, sure. There's an extra
                    key. It was suppose to be
                    six, but there's seven here.

                         SLY
                    We said seven.

                         KEVIN
                    No, no, we changed it to six
                    because the department only
                    had money for six. We
                    never... We must have never
                    told J.

                    KEVIN
No one knows about this baby
except J, and who's going to
believe him. Let's say you
were a drug dealer for real.
I mean, it must have crossed
your mind. If the opportunity
was presented to you, would
you take it? Let's look at
the situation here. We are
sitting with an extra kilo of
pure cocaine. Now, we know
enough people. Gerad comes to
mind. We give him a call, say
can you use this. He says
sure. We drive by his house,
drop it off. He gives us the
money. We have a couple of
drinks. Shoot the shit about
the old days and we go home.
It's so simple, it's stupid
not to do it. On the evidence
sheet, we just put six
instead of seven. Everyone
expects us to put six, so
it's six.

(KEVIN starts to eat a doughnut.)

                    SLY
        Uhm?

                    KEVIN
        Well, what do you think?

                    SLY
        You're joking, right?

                    KEVIN
        You thought I was serious?

                    SLY
        No, I didn't. It's just.
        Forget it.

                    KEVIN
          You know I was trying to
          lighten the mood. What with
          Foster and his angelic story.
          Who does he think he is,
          Christ? I just thought we
          could use a little... Hell,
          it wasn't funny. Okay, how
          about this, a guy walks into
          a bar and sits down. There's
          a monkey sitting at the end
          of the bar...

                    SLY
          Kevin, not the monkey at the
          bar, please. I'm sorry, Man.
          It's just you sound so
          convincing. We do this crap
          too much. This role playing.
          We should be actors instead
          of cops.

                    KEVIN
          You think I want to be like
          J.

                    SLY
          What are you talking about?

(KEVIN puts his hand on his chest.)

                    KEVIN
          I got shot in chest trying to
          put bastards like him away.
          You think I want to be like
          that son of a bitch? Is that
          what you think?

                    SLY
          Kevin?

                    KEVIN
          No, that's what you think?
          You think I'm a bad cop?

                    SLY
          Kevin, I would never say
          that. I wouldn't even think
          that.

                    KEVIN
          Yeah. Well dammit, you better
          not. You just better not.

                    KEVIN
          How was that?

                    SLY
          What?

                    KEVIN
          You think I could play the
          psychotic cop.

(Sly shakes his head.)

                    SLY
          I think you overacted just a
          little bit.

                    KEVIN
          Oh, you fell for it.

                    SLY
          I did not.

                    KEVIN
          I know you, Sly. You thought
          I was going to rip you head
          off or shoot you.

                    SLY
          See, if you pulled out your
          gun, I'd know you were
          serious. No cop pulls his gun
          in a joke. That's how I knew
          you were joking.

                    KEVIN
          I'll let you slide this time.
          Okay, when we drop this off
          at the station, we'll call
          Miki. I think we got some
          left over steaks.

                    SLY
          Steaks?

                    KEVIN
          They were on sell. Catch
          Foster and ask him if it's
          okay to work on the reports
          at my house.

                    SLY
          He'll probably say okay.

                    KEVIN
          Doesn't hurt to check with
          him, nowadays. God may want
          us to go work at the station
          house.

                    SLY
          He'd kill you if he heard you
          talk like that.

(SLY goes out the door.)

                    KEVIN
          I dropped the case off. I
          wanted to get it out of the
          way. Okay?

                    SLY
Foster told me he doesn't
care where we do the
paperwork as long as it's
done by tomorrow. Besides he
says it's a good idea to stay
away from the station right
now.

                    KEVIN
Why?

                    SLY
They're going to be
prosecuting J at our precinct
and he didn't want to risk J
seeing us in our official
capacity. (pause) So, how's
Miki?

                    KEVIN
She's good.

                    SLY
Yeah. Does, uhm, does it
bother you?

                    KEVIN
What?

                    SLY
I don't want to disturb
things by being at your house
tonight.

                    KEVIN
I don't care. By the way what
was that whole my Mother was
saved by an Angel thing with
Foster? Foster once told me
that God moved through his
hands. I didn't know what he
was talking about till I...
Oh well, forget it.

                    SLY
What?

                    KEVIN
You ever see him kill?

                    SLY
Foster?

                    KEVIN
Foster killed the guy who
shot me.

                    SLY
I heard it was justified. He
had just shot you. Foster was
justified.

                    KEVIN
Everything's justified, Sly.
We're cops, we can justify
anything. I was laying on the
floor looking up at the punk
who shot me. My heart's
bleeding. I felt myself.
Well, I felt myself dying.
Foster moves over to the
punk. He takes one hand and
grabs the punk's gun and he
grabs his neck with the other
hand. The last thing I
remember before... before
fading out is hearing Foster

                    snap his neck. I know the guy
                    had just shot me. I... I ...

(KEVIN takes a deep breath.)SLY returns and looks
around. He sits down at the table. He sips his
coffee. KEVIN comes back in without the case. He
sits down at the table.)KEVIN looks around. He
takes the case and goes off stage.)

                         KEVIN
                    I tried to say thank you to
                    Foster, but he just said,
                    don't thank me, thank God.

                         SLY
                    Maybe you just wanted to snap
                    the guy's neck yourself.

                         KEVIN
                    All I'm saying is Foster's
                    not holy and we are
                    definitely not Angels. We're
                    just city employees. Our job
                    isn't even to erase crime.
                    You ever notice how they
                    really push us to make more
                    arrests during election
                    time...

                         SLY
                    It's official.

                         KEVIN
                    What?

                         SLY
                    You are finally a cynic. I
                    had my suspicions before, but
                    now I feel safe in saying my
                    partner is a cynic. You're
                    letting this job get to you.
                    I thought it would be me
                    first, but you're letting
                    it... You're letting it get
                    to you.

                    KEVIN
And you aren't?

                    SLY
Huh? I still seem to think
we're doing good. I don't
think we're some kind of
Angels like Foster does, but
I do believe... Look at J. He
has a warped sense of values.
He went to college, he's from
a middle class family, but
he... He has no morals
though. He's basically
selfish and power hungry and
doesn't care about the
consequences of what he does.
Doesn't care that he's
contributing to the death of
his own people.
He loves it too when white
people buy his drugs. So they
can die from it too. He said,
if he doesn't take advantage
of them, someone else will. I
get sick of stupid people
killing themselves; people
like J taking advantage of
them. The whole drug thing...
I hate this shit.

                    KEVIN
Yeah.

                    SLY
Yeah? That's all you have to
say?

                    KEVIN
I'm tired okay. Miki was...
Look I'm just tired. Let's
just go get the paperwork
done. Now that we've eaten
our coffee and doughnuts,
let's go do our paperwork.
You know, let's go be cops.

(KEVIN goes out the door. SLY looks at the door,
then follows after KEVIN.)
                         (

                                   SCENE THREE:

THE BOCHELLI LIVING ROOM

While the lights fade, MIKI comes out and places
a table cloth over the wood table. She leaves the
stage and returns with four chairs and places
them around the table. She leaves again. MIKI
comes out and places a center piece in the center
of the table.

The door bell rings. She leaves again and returns
and places three beers on the table.

KEVIN walks in the room and SLY is behind him. He
moves toward MIKI, but SLY pushes him aside and
runs over and hugs her first. SLY looks over
MIKI'S shoulder at the table.)

                    SLY
          Hey, beer.

(He lets go of MIKI and goes over to the beer. He
takes a swig as KEVIN finally moves over wraps
his arms around MIKI.)Lights fade.)

                    MIKI
          You're home.

(MIKI starts to take off KEVIN'S coat.)

                    KEVIN
          What are you doing?

                    MIKI
          I'm just trying to help you
          off with your coat.

(She takes off his coat and smiles at him.)

                    KEVIN
          I don't need to be mothered.
          Okay?

                    MIKI
          I'm just trying to be your
          wife.

                    KEVIN
          Whatever. Where's my
          daughter?

                    MIKI
          Our daughter is in her
          bedroom.

(He starts to move to JIMMIE'S room, and MIKI
grabs his arm.)

                    MIKI
          She's sleeping.

                    KEVIN
          Who told you to send her to
          bed?

                    MIKI
          It got late.

                    KEVIN
          I told her I was going to
          tuck her in.

                    MIKI
          Kevin, it got late.

                    KEVIN
          You shouldn't have sent her
          to bed, Miki. Dammit!

(He moves past her and goes off stage.)

                    MIKI
          How'd it go?

SLY
Foster came in like the
calvary and put shotguns next
to our necks before we could
move. He must be training
those cops at some samurai
school. I didn't hear them
until...

(She touches his neck.)SLY looks over to MIKI.
She walks over to the table and sits down. He
sits next to her.)

MIKI
They put a shotgun at your
neck.

(SLY takes her hand.)

SLY
They had to, Miki. We're
safe. It went okay.

MIKI
How is it an okay night when
someone puts a shotgun at
your neck? What if it would
have went off? Mistakes
happen around guns, Sly.
Mistakes happen.

(She takes a deep breath and puts both her hands
on the table, then she takes a drink.)

SLY
You okay? I mean, I never
seen Kevin yell at you.

MIKI
You haven't been around
lately. I guess all your lady
friends keep you busy.

(SLY lets go of her hand.)She reaches out and

puts her hand on his neck. SLY moves closer to
her. He takes her hand.)

                    MIKI
          I'm sorry. What right do I
          have to get jealous of you?

                    SLY
          None.

                    MIKI
          I know. I still can't help
          feeling... I thought you and
          Ann were going to last.

                    SLY
          What did you want? Us coming
          over and having dinner with
          you and Kevin. She asked
          about you. I kept all those
          stupid pictures of us. I
          know, I shouldn't have. I
          don't think of you in that
          way. I was just happy with
          you and I don't want to
          forget that.

                    MIKI
          I don't forget it either. We
          don't have to. We're friends.
          We still love each other...
          Uhm...

                    SLY
          I know what you mean. Look
          Ann wasn't happy when I told
          her that we were good friends
          now. I told her Kevin
          understands. Kevin isn't
          jealous. I think he was at
          one time. He never said it,
          but you know I think he was.

                    MIKI
          He isn't jealous. You have to
          love someone to be jealous of
          them.

                    SLY
          What does that mean?

                    MIKI
          It doesn't mean anything.

                    SLY
          Miki?

                    MIKI
          Sly, please, do not, tonight,
          do not press me on this. We
          were talking about you and
          Ann.

                    SLY
          Miki? There's nothing to talk
          about with Ann. Ann doesn't
          even talk to me. Forget her,
          she's not important. You are.
          Now, what-

                    MIKI
          I'm not... prepared to talk
          about this. Not with Kevin in
          the house. I don't-

(MIKI sits there looking at SLY for a few moments
of uncomfortable silence.)

                    MIKI
          Help me with dinner. We can
          both be barefoot and slave
          over a hot stove.

(She takes a deep breath and remains sitting
there. SLY looks at her.)

                    MIKI
          Sly, you know I want to ask
          you something. How is Kevin
          at work?

                    SLY
          He's Kevin. What do you want
          me to say, Miki? What are you
          looking for here?

                    MIKI
          I'm looking for my Kevin. The
          old Kevin. Doesn't he seem...
          Doesn't he seem...

                    SLY
          Different?

                    MIKI
          Doesn't Kevin seem different.
          I've thought about it for
          months, but... I just wanted
          to say it out loud. I wanted
          to ask you before, but... I
          can't talk to anyone but you.
          You-

(She puts her hand on his.)

                    SLY
          I don't know what to do, Sly.
          When we first got married-

                    SLY
          After you left me.

                    MIKI
After I left you. (beat) I
loved him. Kevin was so
strong. I don't mean
physically. He knew what he
believed in. He knew what he
wanted. It's hard not to fall
in love him.

                    SLY
Yeah.

                    MIKI
He wasn't perfect. I asked
why he was becoming a cop. He
said, to save people. Just
like that. Pure and simple.
When Jimmie was four, she
took some candy from a store.
Kevin didn't beat her. He
just sat her down and said,
you don't steal, you don't
hurt people. That's what he
told her. Kevin... When Kevin
touches me... I'm sorry.

                    SLY
Go ahead. It's okay, I'm over
you.

                    MIKI
Liar. Okay, when he touched
me, I felt his love. Pure and
simple. It was so nice. He
loved me. He was giving me
his full attention.
Everything. He touched me and
he was concerned with making
me feel good. Making me
happy. I never had someone
care so much about making me
happy.

                    SLY
          I know. How is Kevin now?

                    MIKI
          Now? He touches me. We go to
          bed. We have sex. He's not
          there. He holds me sometimes.
          I can't feel him. Physically
          I can, but...

                    SLY
          I know what you mean. It's
          like he's always thinking of
          something else.

                    MIKI
          I know. I want him to be the
          same way he was before he was
          shot.

                    SLY
          It takes time.

                    MIKI
          It's been three months.

                    SLY
          Five. He was in the hospital
          two months.

                    MIKI
          Three months. He's been home
          three months. I gave him time
          to get over it. I'm still
          trying to give him time. Sly,
          I'm a good wife. I know I am.

                    SLY
          I never said you weren't.
          Miki, what do you want to
          say?

                    MIKI
          I'm just saying I'm a good
          wife.

                    SLY
          Miki, you always take... You
          talk in circles. It took you
          a year and a half to break up
          with me. I caught the hint
          sooner, I just didn't...
          Okay, okay. What are you
          trying to say?

                    MIKI
          I do talk in circles.

(She doesn't say another word.)

                    SLY
          I'm going to see what Kevin
          is up to.

(SLY stands up and takes two steps from the
table. He stops when she starts to talk.)

                    MIKI
          He spends a lot of time with
          Jimmie. He always has. He's
          probably reading her a story.
          She likes the Chronicles of
          Narnia. The Lion, the witch
          and uhm, uhm...

                    SLY
          The wardrobe.

(The silence slides back over MIKI again. SLY
turns to leave. Her voice stops him.)

                    MIKI
          I'm thinking I should leave
          Kevin. Jimmie and I should
          leave. Not forever. Just a
          while. He's scaring me, Sly.

(SLY slowly turns back to MIKI.)

                    SLY
          He didn't hit you, did he?

                    MIKI
          No. Well, yeah. I mean
          playful like.

(She smacks Sly gently.)

                    MIKI
          Kevin always hit me playful
          like that. He use to spank me
          and... Oh. You know, just
          Kevin stuff. His joking
          around. It's not that. I've
          always been able to talk to
          Kevin. Now, he doesn't let me
          talk to him. I didn't talk
          around things with Kevin like
          I do with everybody else. I
          could come straight to the
          point. Now, he scares me.

                    SLY
          Do you want me to do
          something? Are you leaving
          for sure?

                    MIKI
          I just want to know before I
          leave. Is something going on
          at work? So, when I leave, I
          just want to know that I'm
          doing the right thing. So, is
          something going on at work?
          Something different.
          Something that's changing
          Kevin?

(SLY shakes his head.)

                    SLY
          Why don't you talk to him?
          It's still Kevin.

                    MIKI
          You haven't heard a damn word
          I said. You want to help me
          cook?

                    SLY
          Okay.

                    MIKI
          Do you want to, or not?

                    SLY
          Yeah. I'll help. Let's
          just...

(She stands. He stands with her.)

                    MIKI
          Come on.

                    SLY
          Miki, just... just give him
          some more time.

                    MIKI
          Well, talk to him.

                    SLY
          Miki?

                    MIKI
          He's yours as much as he is
          mine. Okay. I don't know how
          long I can stand being here
          with him. I don't like this.
          I just want-

                    SLY
          I'll talk to him tomorrow.

(She shakes her head.)

                    SLY
          Okay, can we eat first?

                    MIKI
          We can eat first.

(She leads him to the kitchen. They talk as they
are moving offstage.)

                          SLY
          I heard you had steaks.

                          MIKI
          We got hamburger.

                          SLY (O.S.)
          Hamburger?

                          MIKI (O.S.)
          It's as close to steak as
          we're ever gonna get.

(A moment later. KEVIN comes back on stage with
JIMMIE on his back. She is smiling. He sits her
on the table and looks at the blue pajamas she is
dressed in. He takes a swig of the beer. He looks
back at the "kitchen" and gives JIMMIE a swig of
beer, then takes the can from her as she tries to
drink more.)

                          KEVIN
          Now kiss me.

(She kisses him on the lips.)

                          JIMMIE
          So when Mommy asks how I get
          beer breath.

                          KEVIN
          Beautiful and smart too.

(He sits in front of her. She wraps her arms
around him.)

                          JIMMIE
          I was scared.
                    (She sits back on
                    the table.)

                    JIMMIE
          I know I'm not suppose to be
          scared, but I got scared
          thinking about you and Uncle
          Sly out there with all those
          bad guys. They win sometimes.
          The bad guys. They don't win
          on the cop shows, but in real
          life, the bad guys win. I
          seen them win on tv. The
          news.

                    KEVIN
          Don't watch the news. Come
          on, it's getting late. Uncle
          Sly and I got a lot of work
          to do.

(She hugs him.)

                    JIMMIE
          Can I watch? That's why I
          wore my blue, so I can be a
          good cop and help you.

                    KEVIN
          You want to be a cop?

                    JIMMIE
          Maybe like Lieutenant Foster.
          He sits behind a desk, but he
          comes in when everything is
          over with. He saved you
          tonight... again. Has... the
          bad guys don't beat Foster.
          He's a good cop, you said.
          You say he's the best cop
          there is.

                    KEVIN
          Yeah, he is. He's a good cop.
          I wish I was Foster but I'm
          too selfish. He... I think...
          Jimmie, it's way past your
          bedtime.

(She kisses him on the lips and leaves the room.
SLY comes from the kitchen and places a plate of
hamburgers in front of KEVIN. KEVIN looks as MIKI
comes over and hands him the A-1 sauce. KEVIN
starts to put the sauce on the hamburger. SLY
takes a seat.)

                    KEVIN
          Hey it's chopped steak.

                    SLY
          Miki, when are you going to
          divorce this bum and marry
          me?

(MIKI sits at the table.)

                    MIKI
          What and give up our mad
          passionate affair?

                    KEVIN
          I'd be really upset if I
          didn't know Sly was impotent.

                    SLY
          Ouch. Don't ever say that,
          not even in jest.

                    KEVIN
          Six or seven, Sly?

                    SLY
          What?

                    KEVIN
          I still have the other one.

                    SLY
          You're joking.

                    KEVIN
          Look, I hate to break it to
          you, but I lost my sense of
          humor a long time ago. Call
          the evidence room and see
          what I signed in when I went
          to the station.

                    MIKI
          What are you taking about?

                    SLY
          Kevin thinks we should
          moonlight as drug dealers.

                    KEVIN
          I just get tired of busting
          these punks who are pulling
          down more money in a week
          than we make all year. I'm
          tired of calling hamburger,
          steak. When you went to that
          little diner with J, where'd
          you really go?

(KEVIN stands up. SLY stands and faces KEVIN.)

                    SLY
          It was a diner. He likes to
          eat in diners. He owns the
          place. He owns about seven of
          them.

                    KEVIN
          You know what I own? Nothing.
          We just refinanced our house
          in order to fix it up so it
          won't fall apart. My car
          needs a new exhaust system.
          If...

                    MIKI
          What are you talking about?

                    SLY
          Stay out of this, Miki.
          Please, Kevin tell me you're
          playing some huge practical
          joke and you took all seven
          kilos into evidence.

                    KEVIN
          Your name's on the report,
          Sly, I'll split the money
          with you. Of course, I
          planned to. You and I are in
          this together. We're
          partners.

(SLY pushes his shoulder against KEVIN'S
shoulder.)

                    SLY
          Let's go talk outside.

(KEVIN shrugs his shoulder against SLY'S
shoulder.)

                    KEVIN
          Maybe I don't want to go
          outside.

(SLY pushes KEVIN'S shoulder with his hand.)

                    SLY
          Well, I think you should.

(KEVIN pushes SLY'S shoulder with his hand.)

                    KEVIN
          Well, maybe I don't want to.

(SLY grabs KEVIN'S shoulder.)

                    SLY
          Well maybe I'll just drag you
          outside.

(MIKI stands and moves between SLY and KEVIN. She
uses her hands to push them apart.)

                    MIKI
          Stop it. Just what the hell
          is going on?

(MIKI walks up to KEVIN.)

                    MIKI
          Let me see if I understand
          this. Let me see. There is a
          kilo of cocaine that you were
          suppose to put into evidence
          and you didn't because you
          intend to sell it.

                    KEVIN
          You make it sound so bad.
               (She slaps him.)

                    MIKI
          I didn't marry a drug dealer,
          I married a cop.

                    KEVIN
          Yeah, yeah, you did.

(KEVIN rips open his shirt. There is the scar of
a bullet he took five months ago next to his
heart.)

                    KEVIN
          I got the scars to prove it.
          Doesn't that mean something?
          I took a bullet next to the
          heart. Does anybody remember?
          Does anybody care? What do I
          have to do, die? Huh? You'd
          probably be happy if I died
          that night. I would have died
          an honest cop. An honest cop
          died trying to serve justice.
          A stupid honest cop died
          trying to serve justice. I
          always thought I'd want to
          die like that. I lived. I
          didn't die. I just got smart.
          Shit, you two don't care.

(MIKI sits at the table and doesn't look at KEVIN
who still has his shirt open.)

                    SLY
          We care, Kevin. Kevin, we
          just don't think-

                    KEVIN
          Look, Sly, I know this is
          hard, but I'm not talking
          about making a new career out
          of this. Just this one time
          and it's over. We sell it to
          Gerad. You trust Gerad, don't
          you?

                    SLY
          We grew up with the son of a
          bitch. Yeah, yeah I trust
          him.

(MIKI stands and looks at KEVIN. She walks over
to him and closes his shirt.)

                    MIKI
          I'm going. When this is over,
          I never want to talk about
          this again. Whatever you do
          with the money is your
          business.

                    KEVIN
          This is for us. After Sly's
          cut, we can pay off enough of
          our bills to put us ahead.
          You always said it would be
          nice to be ahead for once.

                    MIKI
          I'm going.

(She looks at SLY, then she leaves the room.)

                    SLY
You planned this all along,
didn't you? You told J to
bring seven keys. How'd you
know he wasn't going to count
the money?

                    KEVIN
Tom Gallons told me he busted
a guy four months ago who use
to work for J. J never counts
the money. If it's a dollar
short, he takes a pound of
flesh. Like Shybock or
Shylock in some Shakespeare
play. I could have said eight
keys but I think six and
seven is an honest mistake.

                    SLY
Honest?

                    KEVIN
I have to go out and meet
Gerad. I'll bring you your
cut back.

                    SLY
How many times have you did
this, Kevin?

                    KEVIN
Did what?

                    SLY
You've did this before. How
many times, Kevin?

                    KEVIN
I... Hell, I'm being open
tonight.

(KEVIN reaches into his jacket. SLY pulls out his
gun. KEVIN stops and lets SLY reach into his
pocket. SLY pulls a bank book from Kevin's
pocket. SLY puts his gun away.)

                    KEVIN
          Don't ever pull your gun on
          me unless you plan to use it.

                    SLY
          I'm not sure I know you.

                    KEVIN
          It's me, Kevin Bochelli, your
          partner.

(KEVIN starts to button up his shirt.)

                    KEVIN
          You know the one thing I was
          thinking about when I got
          shot was. Hhmmm. Me and Miki
          wanted to have another kid
          before I got shot, but we
          knew we couldn't afford it.
          When I got shot, I was
          thinking, " God, I'm going to
          die, and Miki and I didn't
          have another kid cause I
          couldn't afford it.".
          There's... It was just scary-

                    SLY
          My name is on this account.
          There's twenty thousand
          dollars in this account. My
          name is on this account. My
          name.

                    KEVIN
          It's yours. What do you think
          I been doing this past three
          months, getting all this
          money and not saving you half
          of it?

                         SLY
              You... Wait...

(SLY sits down.)

                         SLY
              You made forty thousand in
              three months?

                         KEVIN
              I don't want to go into
              details. I can't do that.
              Let's just say, most of it
              involved passing over
              information to Gerad about
              avoiding certain areas and
              certain deals. I mean, he's a
              friend... I just saw it as a
              favor. I mean, I'd hate to
              see Gerad get shot, wouldn't
              you? Well, wouldn't you?

                         SLY
              When Gerad chose to become a
              drug dealer, he became one of
              "Them". I've used him for
              information, but I knew if it
              came down to it, I'd shot him
              in a heartbeat. There's
              "Them" and there's "Us",
              Kevin. That should never
              change. When I was in that
              room tonight, I was scared,
              but I knew you were coming
              and then it would be you and
              me and "Them". I never knew
              you were one of "Them".
              I'm...

(He puts the bank book in his pocket.)

                    SLY
I'm calling Foster. You know,
when it was just that key, I
was going to let you get away
with it. Just that one little
key of coke. I told myself it
was just this once. You know,
a little pressure from the
bill collectors can drive
anybody crazy. I figured with
tonight going the way it did,
you just got a little off...
I mean it happens.... Still
the main reason I was going
to let you get away with it
was because I ...Kevin, you
know I-

                    KEVIN
I know, Sly. That's why I did
this. I don't think it's fair
for us to be hurting
financially. I kept you out
of this for this long, Sly,
and I swear when I reached
fifty thousand, I was going
to give you your cut. Gerad
owes me some money and with
the kilo, we hit the mark.
Fifty thousand dollars. I can
say we hit the lottery or
some relative left it to me.
I'll keep your share, unless
you want to say, it's your
relative, then you keep it-

                    SLY
I'm only keeping this bank
book long enough to turn it
over to Foster. I guess we'll
have to call in Gerad. I
can't say I won't be sorry to
bust his ass, I just never
thought...

(KEVIN stands and pulls out his gun. He aims it
at SLY.)

                    KEVIN
          Let's talk some more. Sit
          down, Sly and put your hands
          on the table.

(SLY looks at KEVIN, looks at the gun and sits at
the table, with his hands on the table.)

                    SLY
          It's not right, Kevin.

                    KEVIN
          It's just money, Sly. It's
          opportunity. It can take us
          places. You know, I could
          quit with this money. Invest
          a little, pay off some bills.
          Do something else with my
          life where my little girl
          won't have to worry about
          whether or not I'll come
          home. Hey, Jimmie!

(KEVIN places the gun under the table.)KEVIN sits
across from him and points the gun at him.)

                    SLY
          Kevin, don't. Forget it, man,
          I won't do anything.

                    KEVIN
          She's the reason I did this.
          You think I want to be rich.
          Shit, I'm giving half of it
          to you. Jimmie!

                    SLY
          I don't want it.

                    KEVIN
          Keep it. Then you'll be in
          this. Jimmie! You'll be in
          this and you can't talk to
          Foster.

(MIKI comes into the room. She has her coat on
and a suitcase. She puts the suitcase on the
floor.)

                    KEVIN
          Did I ask for you? I asked
          for my daughter. Jimmie!

(MIKI looks over to SLY.)

                    MIKI
          What's wrong?

                    KEVIN
          Nothing, go to bed. What the
          hell is this thing with the
          suitcase.
                 (to Sly))
          What are you two doing,
          running off together, or
          something? Oh hell, who
          cares. I just want... Jimmie.
          Jimmie!

                    MIKI
          Sly?

                    SLY
          Nothing is wrong, Miki.

(JIMMIE comes in the room. She starts to move
toward KEVIN and MIKI grabs her shoulders. JIMMIE
has on her clothes. She looks up at her Mother.)

                    JIMMIE
          I don't want to pack. I don't
          want to leave.

(MIKI is still looking at KEVIN and SLY.)

                    MIKI
Kevin, why are your hands
under the table?

                    KEVIN
Jimmie.

                    MIKI
Kevin come here.

                    KEVIN
Not now.
     (he looks at Sly)
You see how difficult you're
making this.

                    MIKI
Jimmie and I are leaving,
tonight, Kevin.

                    JIMMIE
Mommy, what-

                    MIKI
Hush. Did you hear me, Kevin?
Sly would you drive us to a
motel?

                    KEVIN
Sly has to stay here and talk
to me.

                    MIKI
Okay, so talk to him.
     (KEVIN sighs.)

                    MIKI
Let's go, Sly. You can get
up, can't you? You're a cop,
aren't you?

                    SLY
I don't think it matters to
Kevin. You better go and take
Jimmie with you. I'll be
fine.

                    MIKI
          I'm not leaving here without
          you, Sly.

                    SLY
          Please, take Jimmie and
          leave.

                    MIKI
          Dammit, Kevin you're a cop.

                    KEVIN
          So, what does that make me,
          Miki? Some kind of Angel. I'm
          just a fucking city employee.

(MIKI covers JIMMIE's ears. JIMMIE pulls her
Mother's hands away and looks up to her.)

                    KEVIN
          Jimmie, I'm sorry I cursed.

(KEVIN stands. He places his gun on the table and
pushes it to SLY. SLY takes the gun. KEVIN walks
over to JIMMIE. MIKI takes the little girl and
puts her behind her.)

                    MIKI
          You can't touch her.

                    JIMMIE
          Mommy?

                    KEVIN
          You want to leave? Leave.
          Jimmie stays here with me.

                    MIKI
          You just pulled a gun on Sly.
          You think I trust you.

                    KEVIN
          What?

                    MIKI
          Who knows what you might do
          with Jimmie?

(KEVIN grabs MIKI'S shoulders.)

                    KEVIN
          You bitch. You think I would
          hurt Jimmie? You think I
          would hurt her?

(KEVIN is squeezing the life out of MIKI. She is
nearly crying. JIMMIE steps back from all this.
SLY walks over and puts Kevin's gun under the
couch. He turns back to KEVIN and MIKI.)

                    KEVIN
          I ought to kill you.

(JIMMIE runs up and grabs KEVIN'S arm.)

                    JIMMIE
          Let her go, please.

                    KEVIN
          Go away, Jimmie.

                    SLY
          Kevin, let Miki go and let's
          talk.

(JIMMIE is still grabbing on his arm.)

                    KEVIN
               (to Sly)
          Shut up.

                    MIKI
          Kevin?

(KEVIN lets go of her. MIKI relaxes. KEVIN puts
his hand on her neck. As MIKI gasps for air,
everything goes on at once. SLY moves toward
KEVIN. JIMMIE kicks KEVIN. Without even thinking
about it, KEVIN slams his other arm out at
JIMMIE. When he hits her, she flies across the
room and hits her head on the edge of the table.
JIMMIE collapses beside the table. SLY grabs the
hand KEVIN has around MIKI'S neck and prys his
fingers lose. MIKI looks over at JIMMIE who is

laying still on the floor.)

                    MIKI
          Jimmie?

(She moves over to her. She turns JIMMIE over.
Blood is pouring out of the thick gash in her
head. MIKI looks up at KEVIN. MIKI puts her hand
on JIMMIE'S chest.)

                    MIKI
          She's not breathing, Kevin.
          She's not breathing.

(KEVIN just stands there. SLY turns and looks at
MIKI and JIMMIE. Both SLY and KEVIN remain
frozen.)

                              LIGHTS FADE:

KEVIN and MIKI go off stage. SLY walks over to
the table and sits facing forward.

                              LIGHTS RISE:

SCENE FOUR: AN INTERROGATION ROOM

As the lights rise, SLY is sitting at the table.
He pulls out the bank book and puts it on the
table.)

                    SLY
               I told you the story three
               times. Don't you guys care
               about anything else? Jimmie?
               Huh? She's dead, you know?
               Just like that. A little kid
               is dead and all you want to
               know about is the money.
               About the drugs. Can I at
               least see how Miki is doing?
               You think I care what you
               guys are going to do to me.
               I've interrogated people
               before. I'm a cop, you know?
               I know all the tricks. The

games. The little mind games
you play trying to get
someone to trip up and say
something. Well, you're shit
out of luck here. All I know
is what Kevin told me. He was
different, you know? No, you
don't know.
Before he got shot in the
heart. I guess when he got
shot in the heart, it changed
his heart. I just couldn't
see it. I didn't want to see
it. Kevin always had a
beautiful heart. He's the
reason I joined the force. He
uhm... I just didn't want to
think something could change
him. If I saw his heart, I
would have known it wasn't
Kevin anymore.
Man sees what appears to the
eyes, but God, God sees what
the heart is. I wish you guys
could see my heart. Ohh well.

(He picks up the bank book.)

                    SLY
This is all you see, a cop
with a bad partner and his
name on a twenty thousand
dollar bank account. Okay.
I'm going to tell it to you
again. I'm going to go over
it as many times as you want.
Who knows, you might even get
to see my heart. I pray you
do.
          (SLY puts the bank
          book down.)

LIGHTS FADE

THE END

From Play to TV Movie

NOTES

SEPTEMBER 7th 1998

1. Five minutes need to be added that fit into the story and add to the overall appeal "What Angels Fear". Jim is sending me the complete script (overnight by Wed. Sept 9 1998). The locations have changed in the last segment. I would like to add som interaction with Kevin, Sly and the cops at their job so that you get a sense of how the fit in with the others.

2. Also there is a contradiction: when Kevin sends Jimmie to bed, he gets upset when h comes back and she is asleep. He should want her to be up or either he should be happy t wake her up and Miki should protest about it. "Let her sleep." He always comes back i and wakes her up to let her know he made it back okay.

Neither one of these two problems is a major concern, but will involve a bit of work. I estimat maybe a full day or two should be dedicated to it, then I will talk to Jim and mail it back. would prefer email, that way it can get there the same day.

It could begin, with Foster telling the story about his Mother being saved by Officer Angel Foster then turns to the person he has been telling the story to, and asks him to begin, from the beginning, and says, I think it is in your best interest to tell the truth.

He sets up the video camera and aims it to a man sitting in a chair. The man looks up; he hasn' slept in days. This is Sly Cross.

The Entire Movie Is Sly's Interrogation Sequence.

POSSIBLE DIRECTIONS OF SCRIPT.

ONE POSSIBLE DIRECTION:
It is possible to follow the rhythm of the play and have it begin at the drug bust after the two opening scenes described above and then go take place in Kevin and Miki's house that night as Kevin tries to get Sly involved in what he has been doing.

The end would go back into the Interrogation Room and have Foster dismiss everything Sly as a told him as a lie, and ask him to begin again. Sly gives him the lines in the play about this being the truth, Kevin changing when he got shot in the heart, and how all they see is a cop with a bad partner and his name on a $20,000 bank account. Well, Sly says, I'm going to tell it to you again I'm going to tell it to you as many times as you want. Maybe, you'll get to see my heart. I pray that you do.

FADE OUT

ANOTHER POSSIBLE DIRECTION:

Another direction is to have the Movie lead up to that night in the play where Kevin tries to involve Sly in selling drugs.

Its possible to follow the story from the play but fill in the Story by showing:
- The first time Kevin starts to sell drugs.
- Kevin covering up to Sly and Miki what he has been doing.
- After the drug bust (the same one that is in the play), Kevin decides to bring Sly into the "business" of selling drugs.

The Movie could begin with Foster telling the story about his Mother being saved by Officer Angel. We can see he is inside an interrogation room. Ask he speaks, the flashback occurs. It ends after Officer Angel quotes the Bible to him. Foster looks at the person he has been talking

is Sly. Sly looks like he hasn't slept in days. Foster tells him that the truth is all he wants. Sly says I told you the truth. Foster shakes his head. One more time. Tell it to me one more time.

In the play, it is not revealed till midway into the story that Kevin and Sly are cops, the movie can take the same tone as well if Kevin getting shot is part of a bad drug deal and not during a bust. When Sly tells the story, it seems as if Foster is a cop interrogating a prisoner, not a fellow cop.}

Kevin getting shot could occur with him and Sly "buying" drugs and the Person they are buying from decides to start shooting. They take cover and Foster and others move into the room. Foster has his arm wrapped around the Shooter's neck. He is looking down at Kevin. Kevin sees Foster give him a smile, then break the Shooter's neck. Foster bends down to Kevin. He tells him the ambulance will be there soon. Kevin tries to say, "Thank you." Foster says, "Don't thank me, (looks at the Shooter's dead body) thank God."

This would begin with Kevin's first day back on the job after he was shot. Sly and Kevin are not shown at the police station. They are shown buying drugs. in fact, one of the persons they deal with says to Kevin, "I thought you were dead." Kevin shows him the bullet wound and says, "The mistake the guy made was shooting me in the heart; I haven't had one of those things in years." Kevin and Sly make the buy and Kevin hides one of the keys before giving it to Sly to take with him. Sly says, he is going to drop it off and then maybe come over for dinner.

Kevin says, he has some plans and will meet with Sly later. Kevin finds an old friend of his and Sly's named Gerad Winters. He sells the key to him and lets him know that he will only deal with him. Gerad tells Kevin he is happy he finally came over to the other side. Kevin tells him he is just doing this till he gets back on his feet. Till he gets some bills paid up and he can retire. He doesn't want to get killed this time someone shoots at him. Gerad says, they all say, it's just for a while, till the money starts rolling in, then they're hooked worse than t crackheads. They got to sell more and more. Kevin leaves Gerad's place.

{The rest of the Story depends on how long the Movie is. How long it takes for Kevin to "discovered" and for him to want to involve Sly.}

Kevin selling drugs and hiding it from his family and Sly goes on. Kevin gets assistance from young female cop named Tanya Christie who discovers what he is up to, and doesn't mind, long as he cuts her in on the money. He agrees, and she notices that he is saving half of t money in a separate bank account. "Who's that for," she asks. Kevin says, his Partner. Tan asks is he involved. Kevin says, he will be.

After a date that doesn't go so well, Sly gets a call from Miki that she is worried about Kevi They meet for coffee and she takes Jimmie with her. She doesn't say anything more than s thinks Kevin is seeing someone. She says, he goes out late at night, and when I ask him abor it, he says, its work. She asks Sly, is he working on a new case. Sly says yes.

While they are at the station Sly notices Kevin spending time with Tanya. He follows the thinking Kevin is having an affair, and is surprised when Kevin and Tanya end up at Gerad place.

Sly confronts Kevin about Tanya and he assures her that they are investigating a lead Gerad ha on another drug dealer. Sly tells him, that he should have took him with him instead of th rookie. Kevin tells him that Gerad is more prone to discussing things with women an sometimes brags to them so much, he slips up, and says the wrong thing.

Foster assigns Kevin and Sly to bust Gerad in three days because some of the drugs he is sellin seem to be coming from the police evidence room. They had put trace elements in certain key and found those same elements when they raided one of Gerad's place last week.

Before the raid at Gerad's place, Kevin tries to cut his ties with Gerad, but Tanya won't let him That night, Sly is suppose to have dinner with Kevin and Miki, but Kevin cancels and Mik calls Sly to say he's went out.

Sly goes to Gerad's place and finds Kevin and Tanya involved in a drug deal. He tells Kevir that the bust is going down tonight (things were changed). Kevin and Sly manage to escape but Tanya and Gerad are killed.

Back at Kevin's place, Sly makes a phone call to the station. It looks as if Tanya is going to be blamed as the bad cop. Sly asks Kevin to tell him what happened.

The next series of events follow the play closely with Kevin trying to get Sly involved and showing him the bank book. Yet, when Miki enters the picture and wants to leave with Jimmie, Kevin loses it. Like in the play, and by accident, Jimmie is killed.

's account of the story ends here. He tells Foster he knows the rest. Sly asks to see how ╌mie is doing. Foster lowers his head. "She didn't make it."

╌ almost burst of the room, but Foster holds him back. Sly screams about being held in there, ╌d how all they care about is the drugs and his name being on the bank account. Why don't ╌u talk to Kevin? Kevin isn't talking to anyone, Foster tells him. They have the Doctors ╌king at him now. But, don't worry, when he starts to talk, we'll talk to him. Now, Foster ╌s, why don't you tell it to me one more time. This time, tell me the truth.

╌y says, I've told you eight times. Foster shrugs. We're not leaving till you talk. "Okay," Sly ╌s, "I'm going to tell it once more. Exactly the same. The same way I'll tell it to the jury.

╌vin was different after he got shot in the heart. If I could have seen his heart, I would have ╌own it wasn't Kevin."

╌y holds up the bank book. "This is all you see, a cop with a bad partner and his name on a ╌0,000 bank account. Okay, I'm going to tell it to you again. I'll tell it a thousand times if I ╌ve to. Maybe you'll get to see my heart. I pray that you do."

╌s he starts to tell the story again…

╌DE OUT:

╌THER ELEMENTS IN THE STORY

╌ the play, and Movie, Sly use to date Miki and it comes out that the reason they didn't stay ╌gether is because Sly lied and cheated on her early on in their relationship. Foster focuses on ╌is and replays this part of the video, where Sly says that he loved Miki, but he lied to her. ╌oster asks Sly, why should he believe him if he is the kind of person who lies to a woman he ╌ves.

╌ime should be taken to show how Kevin caters to and adores the time he gets to spend with his ╌aughter Jimmie. Kevin is selling drugs because he wants enough money to retire and he is ╌cared that if he is a cop for much longer, he will be shot and killed. Despite what he has ╌ecame, he does love Jimmie and Miki.

╌riginally the story was set in Cleveland, but it could be filmed in another urban city.

╌ince the police officers spend most of the time doing undercover work, there is little ╌nteraction at the station house with other officers.

DATE	EVENT	NOTES
1 Sept, 1998	Won 1998 Dreambuilders Award	TV Movie to be made based on "What Angels Fear?"
2 Sept 1998	First Meeting with Jim Friedman	Gage Involvement/ Give 4 page Notes based on Original Movie except in this version, like in the play, only Kevin is bad.
9 Sept, 1998	Jim called about adding more pages. So, I sent down a rewrite.	
29 Sept, 1998	Auditions for the Movie at TV 43.	

What Angels Fear? The TV Movie

by
Alex P. Michaels

While the TV Movie is a direct adaptation of the Play,
Additional scenes were added and a few location changes.

FIRST ADDITION

PAGE   SEVEN

SCENE 8

MIKI DOES NOT ENTER THE ROOM AS WRITTEN ON PAGE
7.   THE EXCHANGE BELOW OCCURS AFTER JIMMIE SAYS,
"When are they going to kick us out?"

> KEVIN
> Don't worry baby, I won't let
> anyone kick us out. You know
> what? We're going to get a
> bigger house very soon.

> JIMMIE
> Really.

> KEVIN
> Hey,

He pulls out a scrap of paper and shows her a
house in the heights.

> KEVIN
> that's where we're going to
> live.

> JIMMIE
> It's too big for Mommy.

> KEVIN
> She doesn't know yet. And
> don't you tell her. I'll
> come tuck you in tonight and
> I'll tell you about your
> room.

> JIMMIE
> Tell me now.

> KEVIN
> When I get home.

                    JIMMIE
            What if you don't come home?

He folds up the paper and gives it to her. He
stuffs it in the pocket of her pajamas.

                    KEVIN
            I always come home. Now,

Kevin catches Miki coming into the room

                    JIMMIE
            Are you still going to buy me
            that Ferrari?

Kevin puts his finger to his lips and goes
"Shhhh". He points his head to Miki. Jimmie
slowly looks at her Mother.

                    MIKI
            Jessica?

Jimmie stops and looks at her Mother. Miki
closes the case. She gives Kevin a harsh look.
Miki bends down and puts her hands on Jimmie's
shoulders.

                    MIKI
            Bedtime for you little Lady-

                    JIMMIE
            Daddy, said I could wait up
            for him.

Miki stands up and she looks back at Kevin.

                    MIKI
            Kevin?

                    KEVIN
            I won't be gone long. It's
            no big deal. I just want her
            to be up when I get home.

                    JIMMIE
            Please Mommy.

Kevin wraps his arms around Miki and lays his
head on her shoulder.

                    KEVIN
          Please Mommy.

Miki pats Kevin on his head.

                    MIKI
          Just this once. In fact,
          Jimmie, you can go clean your
          room while Daddy's out.

                    JIMMIE
          Oh pooh.

                    MIKI
          What was that?

                    JIMMIE
          Nothing.

                    MIKI
          Now go to your room.

                    JIMMIE
          Now?

                    MIKI
          No, two seconds ago.

She hugs Kevin.

                    JIMMIE
          See you later.

She moves behind the couch and hugs Miki.

THE REST GOES AS BEFORE, BUT JIMMIE SMILES A LOT
AT KEVIN AS SHE SAYS BYE, AND MIKI LOOKS ODDLY AT
THIS, THEN WHEN JIMMIE SAYS "Don't Forget my
Ferrari, Daddy", MIKI'S EYES DARKEN AS SHE LOOKS
AT KEVIN.

SECOND ADDITION

PAGE 19

SCENE 20

INT. BOCHELLI HOUSE/ JIMMIE'S BEDROOM- NIGHT

Kevin comes in and sees Jimmie asleep. He rubs the top of her head. She doesn't open her eyes, but speaks.

> JIMMIE
> You're messing up my hair.

> KEVIN
> You faker.

She gets up, smiles and wraps her arms around him.

> JIMMIE
> Mommy
> (yawns)
> sent me to bed.

> KEVIN
> Your Mommy doesn't always
> listen to me.

> JIMMIE
> She really wanted me to clean
> my room too.

He looks around her room, which is in some disarray. He starts to pick up some of her things.

> KEVIN
> I can't wait till you get to
> be a teenager.

                    JIMMIE
          Oh, I'll be much neater by
          then. I'll have a bigger
          room.

He smiles at her and sits in a chair by her bed.
He is playing with one of her stuffed dolls. He
sees she is looking oddly at this, and he hands
the doll to her.

                    JIMMIE
          I was scared.

THE REST OF THE SCENE GOES THE SAME TILL IT GOES
DOWN TO PAGE 21.

                    JIMMIE
          I'm glad you're safe, Daddy.

She kisses him. He hugs her.

                    KEVIN
               (Whispering)
          Me, too.

He stands and rubs her hair, messing it up
completely. She gives him a playfully angry
look, then smiles at him. He makes her hair a
little neater, then gives her a smile back and
leaves the room.

NOTES ON PAGE 28   SCENE 22

*I think it might work if some other cops were to
come into the room right when Kevin and Sly are
about to come to blows. Also, when Kevin and
Sly are in the Police Station signing in the
evidence, they should wave or say a brief "Hi"
to some of the other colleagues- yet, because
they are always undercover, they rarely deal
with the other cops; especially the uniform
detectives. A few of the Uniforms and the
Homicide dept. regard them with some sort of
rivalry.*

With the way Kevin and Sly are facing each other, they don't see a PAIR OF HOMICIDE DETECTIVES enter the room. Kevin pushes Sly's shoulder with his hand.

                    KEVIN
          Well, maybe I don't want to.

Sly grab's Kevin's shoulder.

                    SLY
          Well maybe I'll just drag you
          outside.

Sly grabs Kevin and throws him to the door and right into one of the Homicide Detective. Sly freezes. Detective #1 looks at his partner as Kevin steps back from him.

                    DETECTIVE #1
          Narcotics.

                    SLY
          Homicide

Sly and Kevin start to walk to the door. The other Detective is a muscular woman; she pushes right between Sly and Kevin as she walks into the room.

                    DETECTIVE #2
          Excuse me, real cops need to
          use the room.

                    DETECTIVE #1
          Hey Bochelli.

Kevin looks at the Detective give his partner an aspirin.

                    DETECTIVE #1
          I'm a drug dealer; you wanna
          arrest me?

Kevin starts to walk over to him, and Sly grabs his arm.

                    SLY
          You want to waste time with
          these idiots or you want to
          talk?

Kevin turns and walks out of the room. The other
Detectives start to use the equipment as Sly
walks out of the room.

NOTE:

**GO TO SCENE 23 INT. BOCHELLI HOME/ LIVING ROOM -
NIGHT**

*When Miki says "What are you talking about?," on
the bottom of page 28, Sly has not mentioned the
coke yet, he has only said "Kevin thinks we
should moonlight as drug dealers.". For Miki's
line to work, Sly has to tell her about the kilo
of the coke and the evidence room for her to say
what she does on the top of page 29.*

                    MIKI
          What are you talking about?

                    SLY
               (to Kevin)
          You should have all signed in
          that key.

                    MIKI
          I don't think I'm hearing
          this right.

                    KEVIN
          You're not hearing anything.
          Go to bed.

                    MIKI
          I'm not your kid. Don't talk
          to me that way.

Sly grabs Kevin's arm.

                    SLY
               (to Kevin)
     We can still make this right.
     Get the coke, we'll turn it
     in and work this out. You
     know Tommy and the evidence
     boys aren't gonna look at the
     stuff till Monday or Tuesday.
     We still have time-

                    MIKI
     Let me see if I understand
     this. There is a kilo of
     coke that you were suppose to
     put into evidence and you
     didn't because you intend to
     sell it.

                    KEVIN
     You make it sound so bad.

THE REST OF THE SCENE GOES AS BEFORE.

NOTE ABOUT THE GUN ON PAGE 36.

In order for Jimmie to get shot, Sly can not put
the gun under the couch. He has to put it on the
table and when they struggle on page 37, they
(Kevin, Miki, Sly and Jimmie) hit into the table.
If Sly puts the gun under the couch, there is no
way it can be involved.

Or if Kevin still has it in his hand, and he
lowers it but doesn't give it to Sly, then
Jimmie can still be shot. Realizing he pulled a
gun on Sly. Miki runs up to him and smacks him.
Kevin uses his other hand to grab her neck. Then
Jimmie runs up to try and pull him away. She
grabs his arm that is holding the gun). The last
thing we hear is the gun going off and Miki's
hurt voice going "Kevin.".

NOTE: ON PAGE 37/ SCENE 24

Sly should mention something about why they aren't talking to Kevin. My idea was always that Kevin literally stopped talking after this happened. I did want to give more of an impression that Foster has been grilling Sly for sometime about what happened and Foster does not believe a word Sly has said. This could be handled in the exchange when it returns to the Interrogation Room.

Foster leans back. He takes the tape out of the video camera. He writes number three on it, and puts it with two other tapes. He takes a fresh tape out and puts it in the machine.

                    SLY
          Has Kevin said a word?

Foster shakes his head.

                    FOSTER
          You want to talk to a lawyer?

                    SLY
          Do you have a doctor looking
          at him? What's that
          psychiatrist name? The one
          that works here. Uhm-

                    FOSTER
          You want to talk to a lawyer?

Sly shakes his head.

                    FOSTER
          All right. Let's do this
          again.

                    SLY
Some set up line… probably
about J. I've told you the
story. Almost word for word.
The same story. It's the
truth; it won't change.

                    FOSTER
You're consistent; I'll give
you that. I want to hear it
again.

                    SLY
Can I at least see how Miki
is doing?

THE REST OF THE SCENE GOES AS
BEFORE. THIS ADDITIONAL PAGES
     SHOULD CLEAR UP THE
INCONSISTENCIES IN THE STORY AND
ADD THE ADDITIONAL TIME NEEDED.

Epilogue

Dear Friend,

It brought back a lot of memories to reread this story again. I am hoping that soon I can reach out and let you see the TV movie and maybe one day redo this story on the grander scale from the notes here. I'd still like to include that "vision" of the two cops caught in the cross fire which began this story.

I've managed to do other stories and bring Lt. Foster to life in those. Yet, I'm not sure I will revisit what happened to Sly and Kevin and Miki, It seems this story ended with Jimmie and I can't imagine their lives past that.

There is something that I've thought about for years, but I am still not sure of. The entire movie is told from Sly's point of view and at the end of the movie, Lt. Foster has him tell the story again. Sly tells the same story. AGAIN. He has told the same story since before the movie began and as it ends, is about to tell the story again. In the story, Sly comes off as not being involved in what Kevin was doing and in a sense "innocent."

There is the problem. Foster doesn't believe him and honestly I don't know if I do.

I don't honestly know if Sly is telling the whole truth here. Maybe he is the one who was orchestrating the deals and not Kevin. Maybe they were in it together and Miki found out and didn't like it Maybe she was involved and Sly is protecting her. Either way it goes, there is something about the story that makes Foster not believe it. Again, I am not sure if he is telling the truth and that is the main difference in the play and the movie. The play moves straightforward up to the interrogation. The movie begins with the interrogation and everything that comes after is seen through Sly's point of view. He does come off as the "hero" here or a "cop with his name on a bank book" only and only because his partner put it there.

Maybe one day, I'll revisit the characters and find out the truth. Yet, with Jimmie gone, I never went back to any of the characters except Lt. Foster and he never mentions it again. Maybe some secrets are best left kept.

Let me know what you think.

I'd like to talk to you some more, but I have much more to do. Again, I want to thank you for taking the time to read this story and let's talk soon.

Your friend,

Alex

. Other stories featuring Lt. Foster

I said, my Friend, there are other stories with Lt. Foster in it and here is a look at them.

e Darknest Night in Heaven

ief synopsis.

detective places his sanity and his teenage daughter's life in jeopardy when he by-sits a wealthy business man's whorish teenage daughter.

. Foster "opens" this story, but it is not about him. That echoes the TV movie where Foster's st story about his Mother opens that movie. The incidents in "The Darkest Night in Heaven" ppen before "What Angels Fear?"

Red House deadwater"

rief synopsis.

hitman posing as an advertising executive attempts to quit the Mafia and settle own with a nice girl he met.

Scene from "The Darkest Night in Heaven" with Lt. Foster

The Darkest Night In HEAVEN

An original screenplay
By
Alex P. Michaels

"The Darkest Night in Heaven"

FADE IN:

EXT. A WAREHOUSE PARKING LOT - NIGHT

Pair of headlights shine into the white snow. The warehouse is brightly lite, with broken windows and what had been a source of livelihood for nearly two hundred on the banks of Lake Erie is now home to a few hundred rats, and street people with no home elsewhere.

The headlights belong to a black Ford LTD. It sits there as two more cars of the same exact color and make drive up. The headlights are turned off, and the door opens. FOSTER steps out of the car. He is a tall, Black Man dressed in a black suit and wearing a long wool coat. His eyes burn, but his movements are slow, calm and very deliberate.

Almost on cue, the other car doors open. The others are FOUR MEN WEARING WOOL COATS. They look at Foster, he nods, and they start to move toward the warehouse. Before the Four Men Wearing Wool Coats enter the warehouse, they reach beneath their coats and pull out long double barreled shot guns.

The words come across the screen in dark letters among the now falling snow.

SUPER:

CLEVELAND 1983

Foster reaches into his coat and pulls out a walkie- talkie.

Foster looks up to the sky and lets a few snowflakes fall onto his face.

FOSTER
Is it quiet in there?

85

                    NICHOLS (o.s.)
          Quiet as the dead.

                    FOSTER
          What do you see?

                    NICHOLS (o.s.)
          Blood. The lights are on.
          There's about ten of them.

                    FOSTER
          Anybody we know?

                    NICHOLS (o.s.)
          There's ...I can't be sure,
          Lieutenant, but I think it's
          Ray Deeds.

                    FOSTER
          Deeds? Hhhhm. Curiouser and
          curiouser.

                    NICHOLS (o.s.)
          Even with half his face blown
          off, he's still one ugly son
          of a bitch.

Foster puts the walkie-talkie in his pocket and
moves toward the warehouse.

INT. A WAREHOUSE - NIGHT

Foster steps in through the open dock doors.
There is a body laying at his feet. He bends down
to it. It would be wrong to call it a man
anymore, the blood is still pouring out of what
was the man's chest. His face is simply not
there. One of the Four Men Wearing Wool Coats
turns to Foster. This is NICHOLS, a young man who
seems too relaxed around all the dead bodies. He
puts a walkie-talkie in his pocket, and heads
over to stand with Foster.

                    NICHOLS
          Lieutenant.

                    FOSTER
          We'll have to get the
          fingerprints of this one.

                    NICHOLS
          Uzzi. Shotguns. We found
          shells from nine millimeters
          and even a thirty-eight slug.

Foster nods. He looks about.

The warehouse is mostly large open space, and
boxes lined against the wall, with catwalks
above. There are thick cobwebs over most of the
boxes, except one. In front of this box is an
open briefcase with small bags of white powder.
Most of the powder has spilled out from the
bullet holes in the case. Another body is near
the briefcase. This is a huge bulk of a man who
weighed over three hundred pounds. Blood covers
him like a blanket. His fingers are tightly
wrapped around the briefcase.

                    FOSTER
          That seems like a good place
          to start.

Foster and NICHOLS walk toward the huge body. As
they do, it seems to move. It only takes two
seconds for Foster to have his .45 Automatic out
of his coat and pointed at the huge body.

The huge body moves again. Foster looks into the
man's eyes which are wide open. They do not
blink. Foster looks over the man's shoulder and
sees a hand sticking out. Foster puts his .45
away in the same two seconds it took him to draw
the weapon.

Foster turns to NICHOLS.

                    FOSTER
          Give me a hand.

NICHOLS and Foster each grab an arm of the huge
body up under it's shoulder and roll it forward.
The body slams to the floor. The hand that Foster
saw belongs to a MAN IN HIS THIRTIES. He is
covered in blood, and shivering slightly. He
takes in a deep breath of air. His eyes are
closed.

Foster starts to feel the Man's chest. He grabs
his chin and looks into his eyes.

                    FOSTER
          Kim.

KIMWALDEN LAGERFIELD opens his eyes. He is
Scottish, with black hair, and just the
beginnings of a beard. He looks at Foster, then
at the huge body which has now rolled over and is
face up.

                    FOSTER
               This isn't good.

                    KIM
               I can explain.

Foster pulls Kim to his feet.

                    FOSTER
               You will.

Foster looks Kim over.

                    KIM
               I'm not shot.

Foster reaches into his pocket, and pulls out a
pair of handcuffs.

                    KIM
          Foster.

                    FOSTER
               You have the right to remain
               silent.

Foster twirls Kim around, pulls his hands behind

his back, and snaps the cuffs tightly around
Kim's wrists.

                    FOSTER
          If you give up that right-

                    KIM
          I know the speech.

                    NICHOLS
          Who's this?

                    FOSTER
          Kimwalden Lagerfield. He use
          to be my
          partner.

Kim looks down at the huge body. It's eyes are
still open. It's lips have a twisted smile.

**FOSTER APPEARS AGAIN AROUND AN "HOUR INTO THE
STORY"**

**I can't reveal how much more he appears without
giving away the story.**

INT. FOSTER'S LIVING ROOM - NIGHT

The living room is inviting. Foster is sitting in
a leather chair near the couch. In front of the
couch is a coffee table, and at the wall is a
fireplace with a mantle.

Kim is standing by the mantle. On the mantle is a
series of photos in gold frames: Foster, looking
ten years younger, in a Marines uniform; Foster
and Kim in police uniforms standing beside one
another; Foster beside his wife the day of their
wedding; and the last photo with Foster standing
beside a five year old boy who has the same eyes
as Foster. Kim looks at the little boy's grin.

                    KIM
          John's really eighteen now?

                    FOSTER
          Alyssa got straight A's last
          year.

Kim smiles.

                    KIM
          She's always been smart.

                    FOSTER
          Pretty too.

Kim nods.

                    KIM
          Like Liz.

                    FOSTER
          Kim, you were a rotten cop.
          Like one of those little kids
          who can't color within the
          lines so he starts to screw
          up the whole picture.

                    KIM
          Foster, I know I'm right
          here.

                    FOSTER
          You really don't see it, do
          you? You're under
          investigation for murder.

                    KIM
          What?

                    FOSTER
          Not what, who? Ryan Aspir.
          There were three bullets in
          him. The bullet that hit his
          leg is from the weapons one
          of the drug dealers were
          carrying. But, and listen
          very closely, there were two
          shots in his back. One of
          them went right into his
          heart. They were .38 caliber
          slugs. Not one of the drug
          dealers were carrying a .38.
          You know. I need to have your
          weapon.

                    KIM
          Foster?

                    FOSTER
          Give it to me, or I'll take
          it.

Kim reaches behind his back. Foster stands and
walks to stand in front of him.

                    FOSTER
          Slowly.

Kim hands Foster a .38 in a small black holster.
Foster holds the weapon in his hand.

                    FOSTER
          I have to check this against
          the slugs we found. Knowing
          ballistics it should take
          forty-eight hours.

                    KIM
          Alyssa told me, you already
          knew the slugs were from my
          gun.

                    FOSTER
          I want to check with
          ballistics again. If I'm
          going to arrest you, I want
          to make sure the charges
          stick. With Juston Ivory
          protecting you, I don't want
          some lawyer getting you off
          on a technicality.

                    KIM
          Of course not.

                    FOSTER
          Kim, in the next two days,
          I'm going to have to arrest
          you on suspicion of murder.
          Damned good suspicion, and
          answer as to why I didn't
          hold you till I got back the
          first report from ballistics.
          Now, I want you to consider
          telling me the truth.

                    KIM
          I have to go. Seems I don't
          have much time.

Kim walks over to the front door. He turns and

looks at Foster who is holding Kim's .38 and
looking at the photos on the mantle.

                    KIM
          What do you know about S.L.
          Henders?

                    FOSTER
               (still looking at
                the mantle)
          Get out of here while you
          still can.

Kim opens the door and closes it behind him.

Scene from Red House deadwater with Lt. Foster

Red House deadwater

An original screenplay
By
Alex P. Michaels

scene from "Red House, deadwater where Foster talks to a young man named Marcello after shooting. Marcello is the head of the deadwater advertising agency (which is really a front r a crime family). Although it is a fake advertising agency to handle the other fake businesses ed as fronts for illegal activity, Marcello wants to step away from his life and a colleague gets e "agency" to do advertising for a bar called "Red House," whose owner Lisa, Marcello has a ush on. The plans for a celebration at "Red House" are disturbed by "Her," who is from the Family" Marcello really works for.

                    MARCELLO (CONT'D)
          Give me your wallet.

                    JOE
          Why?

                    SHE
          Just shoot him for God's
          sake.

                    MARCELLO
          Don't argue with me. Both of
          you!

Marcello lets Joe reach into his pocket. He hands
Marcello a ragged imitation leather wallet.
Marcello looks at the driver's license. He stands
up and drops it on top of Joe.

                    MARCELLO (CONT'D)
          I know where you live, Joe. I
          know what your wife looks
          like.

Marcello walks to the edge of the alley. Joe is
sitting up. The Woman is still standing there
looking down at Joe. Marcello stops and turns to
her. She tears her blouse.

                    SHE
          When I scream rape, blow this
          fucker away.

She puts a hand in her purse.

                    SHE (CONT'D)
          Or I will.

Marcello looks at her hand as it is starting to
pull a silver handle out of the bag.

                    MARCELLO
          Sorry Joe.

Marcello puts a bullet into Joe's forehead. The
Woman screams rape and throws herself down on the

ground. Marcello runs over to her. He looks down
at Joe. He puts his gun on the ground and reaches
into his pocket. He takes out his cordless phone.

                    MARCELLO (CONT'D)
               Now, I have to call the
               police. God, I hope we own
               some of them too.

                    SHE
               Yeah. You better let me do
               it.

She takes the phone and dials 911. Her voice is
frantic and she is crying to the operator.

He looks down at her purse. The silver handle
seems too long, too curved. He grabs the purse
and turns it upside down; everything that was in
it falls onto the ground. A pack of gum. Paper
clips. A couple of ink pens. A compact. A wallet.
And the silver handle of a hair brush.

Marcello leans back and looks up to see the sun
is beating down on his face.

INT. A POLICE INTERROGATION ROOM

Marcello is sitting with a cup of coffee in front
of him. LIEUTENANT FOSTER is sitting across from
him sipping coffee. Foster is an older Black Man
who at first seems like a kind uncle.

                    FOSTER
               I was surprised to see your
               last name on a police report,
               Marcello. Can I call you,
               Marcello?

Marcello nods.

                    FOSTER (CONT'D)
               You see, we're going to be
               seeing a lot of each other
               from now on. I'm not going to
               hold you. I know that relives

a lot of the tension you're
probably feeling. You did ask
for a lawyer, but we're not
going to let you see one. You
see, Marcello. We aren't
charging you, yet. We're
still investigating the
circumstances of the
shooting. It looks pretty cut
and dried to me. You were
protecting your colleague.
The guy definitely didn't
like you. Your friend Lisa
tells me-

                    MARCELLO
          Lisa is here.

Foster nods.

                    FOSTER
          She came down as soon as she
          heard about it. She told us
          how Joe Micron accosted you
          in her bar a few days ago.
          She told us that she pulled a
          shotgun on Joe more than a
          few times in the past. He
          started fights with her
          customers before and she felt
          that it was just a matter of
          time before someone shot him.
          She was quite helpful. Kind
          of saved your ass, if you ask
          me. I still have problems
          with your colleague's story.
          But this is what I think? You
          want to hear this?

Marcello shrugs.

                    FOSTER (CONT'D)
          I think maybe you were
          getting in a little target
          practice. Oh, I have no doubt
          this guy was an asshole. I

looked him up. He use to
bounce his wife off a wall,
and I lost track of how many
times the police has been
called in to throw this guy
out of a bar. He just
happened to have messed with
the wrong guy. You see, you
put up a good act, but you're
a killer, Marcello. You're a
wild animal and this guy...
Well, no one is going to lose
sleep over him getting shot.
Well, maybe Uhm...

Foster reaches into his pocket and pulls out a
set of photos. He puts them on the table.
Marcello looks to see Joe smiling and holding a
little baby girl.

                    FOSTER (CONT'D)
          I think that little girl is
          the only one who is going to
          miss Joe. You got any kids,
          Marcello?

                    MARCELLO
          You know I don't.

                    FOSTER
          Yeah, you should get married,
          have some kids. You're still
          young. You're rich. You could
          have a normal life. I knew a
          few guys who quit their
          business. They figured it was
          only a matter of time before
          some cop got intrigued with
          them and finally busted them.
          You see, son, I'm intrigued
          with you. It's not good to
          have a cop take an interest
          in you. Not in your line of
          work.

Marcello stands up.

                    MARCELLO
          Can I go home, Lieutenant?

                    FOSTER
          One second.

He reaches into his pocket and lays his card next
to the photo of Joe and his little girl.

                    FOSTER (CONT'D)
          Take my card. Call me if you
          want to talk. Uhm, take that
          photo with you.

                    MARCELLO
          Don't you need it for
          evidence?

                    FOSTER
          It's somewhat unethical of me
          to insist you take it, but I
          like you. Maybe, I feel, you
          can still be saved. I know
          you didn't mean to kill that
          guy. I just want you to think
          about it.

                    MARCELLO
          What if I don't take it?

                    FOSTER
          It was a gesture on my part.
          A gesture that I believe you
          killed this guy in self-
          defense.

There is a knock at the door. Foster goes to the
door and opens it. Marcello looks over Foster's
shoulder to see his Father standing there.
Marcello snatches the photo and Foster's card and
puts them in his pocket. As the door opens, Jacob
begins screaming at Foster.

                    JACOB
          I'll sue this police station
          and take that badge of yours.

This is America, Lieutenant,
a man is allowed certain
rights. Have you forgotten
what your people fought for?

Foster steps back and lets Jacob into the room.
Jacob rushes over and puts his hands on
Marcello's shoulders. He hugs him, then steps
back and looks at him.

                    JACOB (CONT'D)
          How are you, son? You don't
          look okay?

Jacob turns to Foster. Foster claps, then goes
and sits at the table. He looks and sees the
photo and his card are gone. He looks over to
Jacob.

                    FOSTER
          Marcello isn't being charged
          with anything. We are
          investigating the shooting.
          At this time, I feel it
          happened exactly like
          Marcello said. He tried to
          stop the guy from raping his
          colleague. The man hit him,
          then went into his jacket.
          Marcello thought he was going
          for a gun and shot him.
          Marcello's firearm is
          registered and he has a
          license to carry it. He isn't
          being held. You can't sue me
          for talking to him, Sir.

                    JACOB
          Well, thank you Lieutenant. I
          suppose I am somewhat
          distrustful of the police.
          They have always assumed just
          because I am Italian that I
          am linked to the Mafia.
          That's like saying all black
          men are criminals. Well,

Marcello. We should go home
now.

                    MARCELLO
          I have to go to my office. I
          have some work to do.

                    JACOB
          After a shock like yours, I
          think you should see someone.

                    MARCELLO
          See someone?

                    JACOB
          Yes, this is a quite an
          unfortunate incident. The
          timing of it couldn't have
          been worse. I mean, your
          company is coming along so
          fine. You should take a
          vacation. They say, it's best
          to take some time and get
          yourself together after-

                    MARCELLO
          Lieutenant Foster thought I
          might be under police
          observation for a while.
          While the investigation is
          going on.

                    JACOB
          You like talking to the
          Lieutenant? You want to talk
          to him. You think that is
          going to solve the problem.
          Talking to the police never
          solves anything, Marcello.

                         MARCELLO
                         (pushing
                         past his
                         Father)

Lieutenant, didn't you
mention watching me during
the investigation?

                    FOSTER
          Sir, your son and I have
          finished our business here. I
          would like to have him in for
          questioning if needed. I
          would take an issue with it
          if anything prevented my
          talking to Marcello about
          this incident.

Jacob nods.

                    JACOB
               (to
               Marcello)
          As long as you only talk
          about this incident, I have
          no problem. Marcello is
          always safe with me. I think
          you should attend to your
          business, son. Your friends
          are at the bar.

Jacob turns to Foster.

                    JACOB (CONT'D)
          My son is doing the
          advertising for a blues bar
          called the Red House. You
          might want to stop by,
          Lieutenant.

                    FOSTER
          I will. I'm going to be
          keeping a very close eye on
          Marcello. I may never talk to
          him, but I want to make sure
          he is safe.

Jacob pats Marcello's cheek.

                    JACOB

                    Why wouldn't he be safe? Call
                    me, Marcello. We'll talk.

Jacob turns and leaves the room. His footsteps
die out down the hall. Marcello moves to the
door. Foster stands and goes over and slams the
door shut.

                         FOSTER
                    Your Father has a problem
                    with you, Marcello. You may
                    need to talk to me. I could
                    make sure you stay safe.

                         MARCELLO
                    Oh? Even if I knew what you
                    were talking about, and I
                    don't, I'll be fine.

                         FOSTER
                    Will you? You know what I
                    think I just heard here? I
                    think I just heard a man
                    being given a death sentence.

                         MARCELLO
                    You should get your hearing
                    checked Lieutenant. While
                    you're at it, get your eyes
                    checked. I'm not who you
                    think I am.

Starving Artists
2
Working Artists

Made in the USA
Middletown, DE
17 February 2023

24240179R00064